GOOD KNIGHT + BAD KNIGHT and the BIG GAME

For Ev and Katie, who kept the
bladderball in the air.

A TEMPLAR BOOK

First published in the UK in 2018 by Templar Publishing,
an imprint of Kings Road Publishing,
part of the Bonnier Publishing Group,
The Plaza, 535 King's Road, London, SW10 0SZ
www.templarco.co.uk
www.bonnierpublishing.com

Text and illustration copyright © 2018 by Tom Knight
Design copyright © 2018 by Kings Road Publishing Limited

1 3 5 7 9 10 8 6 4 2

ISBN 978-1-78370-812-3

Edited by Katie Haworth
Designed by Olivia Cook

Printed in the UK

Tom Knight

templar
books

was near the end of
summer fair,
the leaves had turned to brown.
Just like our poor old britches
when a dragon came to town.

※

The school had held a jousting match,
we huzzahed for a winner.
Two cousins gripped their jousting
sticks and held on to their dinner.

※

Young Godwin, dressed in
white and gold,
a brave and worthy squire,
and Berkley Paggle,
clad in black,
(whose skills were pretty dire).

They galloped hard, and with a CRACK
young Godwin Paggle got 'im!
Poor Berkley laid down in the mud
and clutched his broken bottom.

But suddenly it all went dark.
A shadow filled the sky.
And all at once, the crowd did GASP;
a dragon had popped by!

It landed with a screeching roar
that turned our legs to jelly.
Its fearful eyes did seem to say,
"Yummm! Get inside my belly."

ut Berkley sprang
up to his feet
and showed no signs of fear.
He grabbed his catapult and cried,
"Oi, Big Nose, over here!"

※

Young Berkley fired, the
dragon roared,
the crowd let out a sob.
The stink bomb whizzed right
through the air,
and down the dragon's gob.

※

A mighty bang and then a smell
to curl your very toeses;

nobody could decide whether
to cheer or hold their noses.
❊
But cheer we did, the
dragon had been
put right through
the wringer.
Brave Berkley
Paggle saved
the day;
the fearsome
stink-bomb flinger!

Dear Diary,

HUZZAH! School on the morrow!

I just can't WAIT to tell Berk what I found! It's weird that I haven't seen him much this summer though. I reckon he's been keeping a low profile after defeating that dragon. Zooks, I wonder how he's feeling after all that.

WP

1.

THE NIGHT BEFORE SCHOOL

Berkley Paggle was feeling very odd. It was the last evening of the summer holidays, and he was lying in bed staring at the stone ceiling with a strange sensation in his tummy. It was like thousands of butterflies were tickling his insides. And then he realised what the weird feeling was.

It was happiness.

For the first time in his entire life, Berk was excited about going back to school.

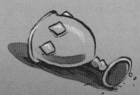

Normally the night before the first day of term meant hose[1]*-dampening fear. Berk would try anything to get out of going. This time last year, he had covered his face in slime from the moat and burst into the castle hall.

Clutching his tummy, Berk staggered into the middle of the room.

"I . . . feel . . . a . . . bit . . . bubonic[2] . . .!" Then he flopped about on the floor, and with a blood-curdling death rattle, lay still on the rug.

Berk's mum had just smiled.

*Go to page 158 to look up any words with a number beside them.

Go and wash that slime off your face
and get back into bed," she said. "I'll
come and tuck you in."

"Impressive spasming, son," said his dad.

But this term was going to be different.

Now he, Berkley Paggle, who everyone had called Bad Knight for as long as he could remember, was a HERO.

It had all started when Berk's cousin had come to stay. Godwin Paggle was good at EVERYTHING. Sword fighting, jousting – even tapestry making. He could play the lute and he was always helping around the house. Godwin was PERFECT,

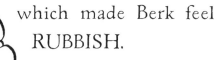

which made Berk feel RUBBISH.

Berk had put all his energy that term into making a catapult. Maybe he could just ping Godwin all the way home.

But the catapult came in very handy when Godwin and

Berk had to face each other in the end-of-term jousting tournament.

Godwin had defeated Berk easily, but while Berk was lying on his bottom in the mud, a DRAGON flapped into the school grounds. Berk had grabbed his catapult and fired a troll-breath stink bomb right into the dragon's gob.

The whole school had seen him defeat the dragon, and Godwin had written a soppy ballad about it, which all the bards were singing.

Berkley was no longer a Bad Knight.

He was a LEGEND.

2.

LORD DE BEEF

Godwin and Berk made their way into the great hall for assembly. The room buzzed with excited chatter.

Sir Donnick Remarque, the deputy headteacher, trotted onto the stage, brandishing a long golden bugle.

※

Sir Donnick was the smallest, vainest knight on the teaching staff. He always wore long pointy shoes and puffy hats with enormous feathers. In his youth he had never been allowed to go into battle because the other side just laughed at him, and knights liked to be serious when they were fighting. Instead he was given the job of 'official bugle blower', which seemed to keep him happy.

PARRAAAAARRRPP!!

Silence fell over the hall.

"THANK you," said Sir Donnick.

A loud, farty noise echoed round the hall
in reply, and someone giggled. Sir Donnick
glared at Berk. Why did everyone always
think he was responsible for this sort
of thing?

Sir Donnick took his place amongst the

rest of the teachers to make way for the enormous figure of Lord Cedric de Beef, the headteacher.

Lord de Beef had once been the most famous knight in the kingdom and mummers[3] re-enacted his famous battles all across the land. He had once singlehandedly stopped the ogre uprising of the Mudgrump Marshes with just a piece of string and a minted lamb chop. When Lord de Beef grew weary of fighting, he dedicated his life to teaching the code of chivalry[4].

"Well met my little fauntkins[5]!" he boomed. "I pray thou all hadst a chivalrous summer? Mine eyes doth grow moist at thine eager little faces, staring up at me like blank platters, ready to be piled high with hot, buttery knowledge!"

Somebody snorted, and Sir Donnick Remarque blew a sharp blast on his bugle.

"Ahem, thank you Sir Donnick. Now my eager lambkins, prithee lettest me make two small announcements. I shan't squiddle⁶.

"Firstly, this year shalt herald the very first inter-school bladderball match. Our honourable opponents shall be St Splendids School for the Financially Gifted. HUZZAH!

"Now, as thou knoweth, we had a rather eventful time last term . . . "

"This is it," hissed Berk, digging Godwin in the ribs.

"The school jousting tournament very nearly ended in disaster thanks to a particularly unpleasant dragon. But we were saved by one resourceful pupil."

The headteacher looked at Berk, who instantly turned bright crimson. "Wilt thou joineth me in the heartiest of huzzahs in honour of the school hero, BERKLEY PAGGLE!"

Lord de Beef boomed "HUZZAH!" again at the top of his mighty voice, and soon the hall rang with applause, cheers and whoops. Even Sir Donnick Remarque was clapping, although he looked as if he had just smelt something very unpleasant.

3.

BUDDIES

Godwin and Berk made their way into the school courtyard. Everyone seemed to want to slap Berk on the back or shake his hand. Several people even drew selfies with him on their stone tablets.

"This is the best first day of school EVER!" said Berk to Godwin.

When Godwin had been sent away to begin his knighthood training with his Uncle Gregory and Aunt

Isobel, he hadn't wanted to leave his parents at first. But Berwick, Godwin's father, insisted that if Godwin wanted to be the chief of their village, just like he was, then he would first have to learn the knightly skills of horsemanship, fighting and, above all, chivalry.

Berwick sent Godwin to learn from his brother Gregory, a great knight himself, and Isobel, a famous horserider. Godwin would also attend Silveroaks, the best knight school in the land.

The only problem had been Berk.

No matter what Godwin did, his cousin seemed to despise him.

But that all changed after Berk had defeated the dragon. And now Godwin felt like he had found a true friend.

"Berk! Oi, Berk! Wait for me!"

A small boy in a colourful robe burst through the crowd. "Berk! Didn't you hear me—?"

The boy suddenly tripped and fell. His glasses shattered. Godwin helped him to his feet. "Zooks!" said the boy.

"Not another pair! Mum's gonna put my head on a stick!"

"Hello Warrick," said Godwin.

"Hi Warrick," said Berk. Godwin noticed that Berk didn't look pleased to see his friend, which was funny – they'd hung out together lots last term.

Warrick Pitchkettle stuck his glasses back on. "Berk! Guess what? I found a sp—"

"Wassup Berserker!"

A tall boy was striding across the courtyard. He was flanked by an even larger boy with a shaved head, and a bored looking, skinny girl. Behind them prowled two identical twins, their eyes hidden by waterfalls of black hair. They growled at anyone who looked at them.

"J-J-Jax R-Rutterkin!" stuttered Berk. Godwin thought he seemed nervous. Jaxon Rutterkin was the coolest kid in school, and captain of the bladderball team, the Silveroaks Squires. Last term Godwin had rescued Berk and Warrick several times after Jax had shoved their heads down the privy[7], but now here was Jax, smiling at Berk and holding his hand in the air.

Berk looked very confused.

"He wants you to slap it," whispered Godwin.

Shaking slightly, Berk slapped Jax's hand, hard. Jax winced, then pumped his fist in the air. "Now THAT is what I'm talking about! That's why you're Berk the Berserker now! You frushed[8] that dragon last term."

Godwin watched Berk's mouth flap open and shut like a fish.

"Meet the crew." Said Jax, pointing a thumb at the giant man-boy beside him. "This is Big Wesley, and this," he pointed to the bored looking girl, "is Gwendoline Trusskettle. And these two killbucks⁹ are the La Forge twins, but I wouldn't get too close if I were you."

Suddenly, the bell for class rang.

"Some of us are going down to the

wagon stop after school tomorrow," said Jax. "See you there Berserker." He didn't ask Godwin to come.

"Errr, right, yep. Laters!" said Berk. Then he and Godwin sprinted for class.

From behind the pillar where he'd been hiding, Warrick watched them disappear into the crowd.

"But I needed to tell you something important . . ." he muttered.

Dear Diary,

Bit of a rubbish first day. Berk was too busy trying to impress Jax Rutterkin to listen to me. Never mind, I'll pop round to his castle tonight. What's the point of having a huddermudder[10] if you cant share it with your best friend?

WP

4.

A FRIEND UNHINGED

"Tonight's stew was an absolute triumph, Aunt Isobel," Godwin said as he finished the last bite of his trencher[11]. "The hint of sage was a masterstroke!"

Usually Godwin's after-dinner chats made Berk want to throw up, but he was in a very good mood this evening.

"And how was school today?" asked Gregory. He was picking pieces of lamb out of his beard and popping them into his mouth.

"It was the best day ever!" said Berk. And it had been – it had felt amazing having all the attention on him for once, instead of oh-so perfect Godwin. He went on, "You'll never guess who wants me to hang out with him after school tomorrow!"

He paused for dramatic effect and his family looked enquiringly at him.

"Jax Rutterkin!"

"Jax Rutterkin?" Scoffed Patience, Berk's little sister. "He thinks you're a complete plague-sore!"

"Not anymore troll-face!" sneered Berk. "Now he thinks I'm a proper killbuck! He calls me Berserker."

Patience spat her milk across the table. "Berserker? Haha! Well I suppose it's an improvement on your real name, BERKley."

"Stop your fadoodle[12]," said Isobel. "Your brother was very brave, and he deserves people being nice to him for a change."

She looked over at her husband, who was still rooting around in his beard for bits of food.

"For goodness' sake, Gregory, if you're still hungry there's apples in the bowl."

Gregory eyed the fruit suspiciously. But

before he could protest, the doorbell clanged.

"I'll get it," said Berk.

Berk cranked the heavy winch, and the portcullis clanked upwards. Behind it, stood Warrick Pitchkettle.

Warrick and Berk had been best friends since they started school, mainly because nobody else would hang out with them. Warrick lived with his mother, Hildred, in a tumbledown cottage on the edge of the woods.

All the other kids thought Warrick was a total fopdoodle[13]. He had curly red hair, and thick glasses that magnified his eyes and made him look a little barmy.

Warrick had a twin sister called Willow, but she had gone somewhere with Warrick's dad a year ago. Warrick boasted that his dad was a great wizard, and that he and Willow were

36

doing something extremely important, but Warrick was always making up stuff. Besides, there was a rumour in the village that Warrick's parents had split up. Berk had often heard them arguing. He just wished Warrick would be honest with him.

Warrick was hopping from foot to foot with excitement. "Sorry to come round so late! Were you having your tea? Me and Mum had boiled cabbage with newt bits in it – it was 'orrible. My tummy feels a bit squiffy, but I've got something really important to tell you!"

The words spilled out in a breathless stream.

"I was trying to fix our privy to help Mum. It's stopped flushing so we've been

doing our business in the compost heap, which is full of hedgehogs – my bum's like a pin cushion. Anyway, I looked in the top where the flusher is and I found this weird old spell book wrapped in a pair of my dad's old leather britches!"

But Berk was distracted. He wanted to go and hang out on the battlements with Godwin. They had recently designed some new arrow fletching, and Berk was keen to get some target practice.

"Look, Warrick, now's not a good time."

Warrick looked crestfallen.

"But . . . but what about the book? I think it belongs to . . . "

But Berk wasn't listening.

"Warrick, I'm busy. I'll see you
tomorrow at school." and before Warrick
could say another word, Berk shut the
portcullis with a heavy clank.

Dear Diary,
I looked at the book tonight without Berk, since that fopdoodle is clearly FAR TOO busy and important. There is this name that's repeated over and over: Kapp Zlock. I wonder who that it? I'll bet it's whoever has got Dad and Willow. Mum won't talk to me about it but I reckon they're in trouble and they need me to save them.

Wp

5

THE WAGON STOP

The next evening, Berk and Godwin walked to the village.

"What did Warrick want last night?" asked Godwin.

"Oh I don't know, he was crowing on about some book he'd found."

Berk was nervous about meeting Jax and the others so he'd asked Godwin to come too.

VILLAGE

The gang were sure to be impressed with Godwin's knight skills.

When they got to the wagon stop Jax, Big Wesley, Gwen and the rest were squeezed inside.

"Here he is!" crowed Jax, ignoring Godwin again. "Berk the Berserker!"

Berk raised a hand to wave.

"Well met my fine fellows!" said Godwin cheerfully.

Berk glared at his cousin, who smiled innocently back.

"So, stink-bombed any dragons lately?" said Jax.

"Erm, no." Berk suddenly remembered that he had to be more Berserker-y, so he made an effort. "B–but if I did see one, I'd fire it at the moon! Peeeeoiiing!"

Jax and the gang seemed to love this. They began dancing round the wooden shelter wielding imaginary swords.

Big Wesley cupped his hand over his mouth and made drum noises, and

Gwen joined in with some surprisingly
tuneful oooohs and yeaahs. Jax leaped
onto the seat and began to
make up a rhyme.

They call him the Berserker,
and if you're a dragon you know
he's gonna hurtcha.

Berk's face grew hot with happiness.
Godwin, who had been cheerfully
clapping his hands said, "Mayhaps I
could sing a ballad?"

Berk froze. Surely Godwin wasn't going
to embarrass him?

But Godwin had began to sing:

I knew a lovely maiden,
who had a lovely nose,
as pointed as the mountaintop,
as scarlet as a . . .

SPLAT!

A rotten scroggling[14] exploded on the wall right next to Godwin's head.

"Get him!" shouted Jax.

"Come on now!" said Godwin. He looked at his cousin hopefully "Berk?"

Berk tried to say something, but Jax and the gang couldn't

hear him over their laughter.
Godwin turned and fled, rotten
apples whizzing past his ears.

Dear Diary,

Zooks, this spell book is confusing. It's full of weird runes.

I've got to be careful though. Mum'll kill me if she finds out I've been doing magic. She hasn't allowed any since Dad and Willow went missing. I just have to find Kapp Zlock. The answer is in here somewhere, I know it.

WP

6.

BANG!

One day at lunchtime, Godwin was in the school privy, washing his hands thoroughly (as usual). Suddenly there was a loud BANG from one of the cubicles. This sort of thing often happened. The plumbing was very dangerous, and the privy was just a large pit that everything fell into – sometimes even students.

Godwin gawped in horror as green smoke began to pour out from under the door. Suddenly it burst open, revealing a terrifying figure. It was black with soot and its hair was smouldering. Godwin thought it was a ghoul. "Stay back foul demon spawn, or I shall send you back down the privy from whence you came!"

BANG!

The ghoul clattered straight into Godwin and fell on the stones with a squeaky "Ooof!"

"Warrick?" asked Godwin.

"Erm, I wouldn't go in there if I were you," said Warrick. "I've done a bad spell!"

And then he disappeared into the corridor, clutching an old book.

Godwin peered into the toilet cubicle. When the smoke finally cleared, he noticed an odd scorch mark on the wall. It was in the shape of a horned head with a huge, toothy grin.

He started to back away when he felt something crack. Under his foot were Warrick's glasses, both lenses broken.

Dear Diary,
I think I know how to find Dad
and Willow! Listen to this:

A RING OF ROPE, A TOADSTOOL SPORE,
SIX CHAMPIONS WITH HELM AND GLOVE
WILL SUMMON UP MY PORTAL DOOR
(BUT SHUT IT AFTER, THERE'S A LOVE).

Zooks, where am I going to find
six champions? I wish Willow was
here. She'd know what to do.

WP

7.

THE SHACK

odwin was walking down the lane to Warrick's house. He kicked angrily at a stone, which turned out to be a bit of horse poo.

CAWK!

"Oh, zooks."

Godwin was in a bad mood. Berk was acting like a real braggart[15]. All he wanted to talk about was Jax and the gang and he seemed to have forgotten that they had bombarded Godwin with rotten apples.

And now, instead of going with Godwin to see if Warrick was OK, Berk was going back to the wagon stop. The knightly code of chivalry didn't seem to mean much to Berk, but Godwin was determined to stick to it, even if he did have poo on his boot.

Around the next bend, Godwin saw a tumbledown shack. A tree sprouted through its thatched roof, and rooks screeched in the branches. Godwin knocked at the door and a few seconds later a suspicious eye peered out.

"We have all the newt's eyes we need, thank you!" And the door slammed shut.

Godwin called through the keyhole. "I'm a friend of Warrick's from school."

The door creaked open, revealing a small, tired looking woman with the same red hair as Warrick. Godwin bowed with a flourish. "Godwin Paggle, at your service, m'lady."

The woman smiled then. "You must be Berk's cousin."

"That's right. I came to give Warrick his glasses back."

"My name's Hildred – I'm Warrick's mum. You've just missed him – he's gone to the forest to pick mushrooms for our bellytimber[16]."

Just then, behind Hildred, there was a popping noise, and Godwin saw the lid fly off a large cauldron.

Hildred ran to stir it. Godwin could just hear her mutter under her breath, "Cooking was much easier with magic."

She called over her shoulder to Godwin. "Look, could you go and find Warrick for me and hurry him up? I need his help!"

Godwin bowed deeply, "Fear not, Dame Pitchkettle! I'll gladly undertake the quest."

Then he ran towards the woods.

8.

COOL KNIGHTS ON THE BLOCK

CLONK!

"Nice shot, Berserker!" shouted Jax. Berk and the gang were hanging out behind the local tavern. They were firing stones from slingshots at pictures they'd painted of their teachers on the slop-bins. Berk had just scored a perfect bullseye on Sir Donnick Remarque.

"We're definitely gonna beat St Splendids this year at the bladderball match," said Jax, his conker hitting Sir Cumference, the deathly dull magimathics teacher.

CLUNK!

"Yeah, you'll whoop 'em for sure," said Berk.

"What do you mean 'you'?" said Jax. "You're on the team too. Coach is well up for having the Berserker play for us!"

"M-m-me? B-but I've never played bladderball in my life!"

Bladderball was the most popular game in the kingdom, but Berk had never understood why people got so excited about it.

"Honestly Jax, I don't even now how to play!"

"It's simple! Look . . ."

Jax got a stick and drew a bladderball pitch
in the dirt. "The aim of the game is to get a
many points as possible," he said. "And you d
that by hitting the quintains, which are thos

BLADDERBALL

PRIME QUINTAIN.
worth 100 Points
If we hit this we WIN!

ORDINARY
QUINTAIN
10 Point

things in the middle of the field." He said a lot of other stuff too and after a while, Berk thought he was getting the hang of it.

RULES

The Players

SLINGERS

Have to hit the quintain with the bladderball.

SUGGERS

Have to stop the other team's slingers

GRAND QUINTAIN 50 Points

Berk stared at the strange marks. Could he really make it onto the team? He'd never been good at anything before. He looked at the scuff mark where his stone had hit the drawing of Sir Donnick. Maybe he could do this.

Dear Diary,

I found a spell in the book that's given me an idea. It's for ree . . . reantima . . . rhianna . . . bringing dead stuff back to life. Dad said there's LOADS of famous knights buried down in the old crypt. I bet I'll find my six champions there.

WP

9.

THE CRYPT

Godwin was deep in the woods and he hadn't found Warrick yet. He was cold and scared, but he knew he had to be brave.

Pushing through the branches, he found himself in a clearing where a ruined church stood. Godwin heard a loud fzzZZZzz!

followed by a CRACK. Then he saw a head of red hair disappearing downwards in a cloud of smoke.

"Uh-oh," thought Godwin.

Amongst the moss-covered tombstones was a large stone slab, which was split in two.

Behind it, a set of stone steps lead into the darkness. Godwin took a deep breath and followed Warrick underground.

✖

At the bottom of the staircase was a vast chamber lined with stone tombs. Warrick was standing in the middle with his back to Godwin. In his hands was a large book.

Godwin was about to call out when Warrick began to chant:

Though thee thought thine work was done,
heed me now, oh rested bones.
Where once was flesh, there now be none,
so stir ye from your sleeping stones.

Godwin heard a rattling from inside the tomb he was standing beside. Suddenly the lid slid off, and the strangest thing he had ever seen slowly emerged. It was a skeleton, but it was as if somebody wearing a blindfold had put it together. Random bones splayed out from the ribcage, and it walked like an elderly crab.

Godwin clamped a hand over his mouth so he didn't cry out, and ducked behind the tomb. The crypt was now full of the sound of stone lids scraping open, and bizarre arrangements of bones were clambering out. They moved towards Warrick, but they fell apart before they reached him.

Warrick picked up his book and fled. Godwin followed him up the stairs, but by the time he reached the top, Warrick was already running through the woods towards home.

Dear Diary,
Well I tried the spell
down in the crypt and it
was a complete failure!
Now how am I going to
find six champions?

WP

10.

BLADDERBALL

"Berk, Get up!"

Berk was lying with his face in his pillow. Someone was yelling at him, and he'd had the most awful dream. He had been standing in a muddy field trying to catch a bladderball, but

every time it was just within reach he got trampled into the mud. "Get UP Berk! NOW!"

Berk lifted his face just in time to see a dark object flying through the air.

This was no dream!

He leaped up. "Run!" shouted Jax.

Desperately, Berk leapt for the ball, caught it, and ran.

Glancing over his shoulder, he saw Big Wesley close behind.

Berk tripped over his boot and rolled through the mud. The ball flew out of his hands, bounced off Big Wesley's head, and hit a quintain.

"That was some extraordinary bladderball, Paggle!"

Berk wiped the mud out of his eyes and saw Sir Kitt Trayning, the games teacher, grinning down at him.

Before he could explain it had been an accident, Jax grabbed the bladderball and raced towards the centre of the pitch.

"Nice one Berserker!" he called over his shoulder.

Berk gritted his teeth and followed.

The quintains were a wooden target that

was attached to the end of a rotating arm on top of a pole. A heavy sandbag hung from the other end of the arm, and each time the bladderball struck the target, the whole arm swung around wildly. Gwen and the La Forge twins expertly ducked the sandbag each time they ran past.

"That big one at the end of the pitch is the prime quintain," explained Sir Kitt to Berk. "It's worth 100 points. If you strike that target with the bladderball we'll be well on the way to winning."

Berk stared up. The tiny target seemed to disappear in the clouds.

"I couldn't even hit that with my catapult!"

"Don't swerk[17] it Berserker!" said Jax. "We've got a plan!"

Sir Kitt proudly unveiled a chalkboard on which a series of complicated diagrams were drawn. "Jax and I have devised a brand new move. We call it 'The Paggle Pulcifier'."

"The WHAT?" spluttered Berk.

"We've based it on your dragon vanquishing technique! Basically, Jax and Big Wesley are the catapult. They link arms and plough through the

St Splendids
team. Then
you run up
their backs, they
leap into the air, and
you lob the ball at the
prime quintain.

Tada! 100 points! And Berkley Paggle is the school hero. Again!"

Berk began to think that being a hero wasn't all it was cracked up to be. He was so nervous when they tried the Paggle Pulcifier that he managed to trip everyone up.

"Not to worry, I'm sure we'll get there," said Sir Kitt Trayning, but he looked worried.

Berk had not noticed the small figure lurking in the shadows of the stalls. Warrick had been watching, and was beginning to get an idea.

Dear Diary,

Why didn't I think of it before! There's six players on a bladderball team, and whoever wins will be champions! I want Berk's team to win; it'll serve him right for ignoring me. They're just going to need a bit of help . . .

NP

SILVEROAKS SQUIRES

·G. TRUSSKETTLE· ·B. WESLEY· ·J. RUTTERKIN· ·B. PAGGLE·

·T. LAFORGE· ·P. LAFORGE·

11.

BULLSEYE

THWWAAACK!

Godwin's arrow pierced the centre of the target and quivered.

"Excellent shot as usual, Paggle," said Sir Donnick Remarque, as he walked down the line of pupils with his hands behind his back. Berk fumbled with his arrow as he tried to nock it to his bowstring. Archery had become one of his favourite lessons, but he had other things on his mind this afternoon.

"Look Godwin, I really haven't got time to worry about Warrick right now. Jax has got me practising every day. I'm so sore I can barely draw this bow."

WHIIIIZZZZ!

Berk's arrow went over the target, and disappeared into the clouds.

"Oh dear," sneered Sir Donnick. "I hope you'll do better than that against

St Splendids, Paggle."

Berk's face turned bright red.

Godwin nocked another arrow. "But I think he's in trouble. We need to help him before he conjures something he can't control."

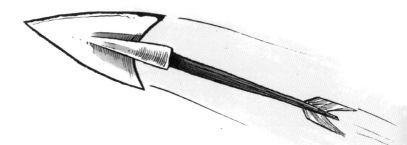

THHWOOCKKK!

Godwin's second arrow split his first one right down the centre.

Berk's face grew redder still. Why was Godwin always so good at everything?

"What an enormous pile of troll

droppings!" he snapped. "Warrick Pitchkettle couldn't conjure his way out of a sack of manure! Besides, I've got more important things to worry about! I'm playing in the school bladderball match next Friday in case you'd forgotten!"

WHHEEEEE!

Berk's arrow span wildly off to the side. Now Godwin was angry too. "I know you've got a lot on your trencher, but I need your help." He pulled back the bowstring. "What if he really hurts himself?"

THWWUNK!

Godwin's arrow pierced the target so hard that it nearly

came out the other side.

"Very impressive," drawled Sir Donnick. "Looks like Sir Kitt Trayning picked the wrong Paggle for the bladderball team."

Berk's face went purple. "It's alright for you!" he hissed at Godwin. "You don't have to try at anything. But I do!"

He pulled back his bowstring and focused on the centre of the target. He was shaking with fury.

THHWACCKK!

The arrow flew wide and skimmed the top of Sir Donnique's head, pinning his wig to a tree trunk.

Dear Diary,

I've found a spell in the book that seems to be important - it's circled twice with red ink. It says:

BALL OF FLESH, A HUMAN TOOTH,
NOT WIZARD SPELL OR KNIGHTLY SWORD.
THEN SPEAK YE ONE UNSPOKEN TRUTH,
TO HOLD FOREVER BACK THE HORDE.

I don't know what it means, but I can't worry about that now. It's the big game tomorrow!

12.

BACK TO THE SHACK

The last few days hadn't been great for Godwin. Berk had been in detention every afternoon since the archery lesson, and Godwin had been worrying.

He'd been trying to put all thoughts of Warrick out of his head – Warrick was Berk's friend, not his! But Godwin knew he couldn't just do nothing, so he'd decided to talk to Warrick himself.

He was on his way to Pitchkettle Cottage now, but, as he rounded the corner, he saw a small, tattered book lying on the ground. He picked it up and looked at the cover:

Warrick Pitchkettle's top-secret diary. Do not read (unless you are Warrick Pitchkettle).

Godwin knew that a true knight would never read somebody's secret diary. But then again, he wasn't a true knight yet, just a squire and this might be his best chance to help. What would Berk do?

Ten minutes later, his hands shaking, Godwin closed the book and leaped up from the tree stump he had been sitting on. "I have to stop Warrick!" he cried, and he sprinted towards Silveroaks School.

13.

THE BIG GAME

In the players' pavillion at the bladderball pitch, Berk was holding his helmet and trying not to be sick.

"Don't be carked[18] Berserker, it's just first-match nerves," said Jax.

Suddenly the harsh sound of Sir Donnick's trumpet rang out. The tournament was about to start! Berk's stomach did an enormous lurch. The three bowls of high-protein vegetable pottage[19] Jax had made him eat that morning sprayed into his helmet.

"This is it, Berserker!" said Jax, and as he ran past he grabbed the helmet and stuck it on Berk's head.

As the Silveroaks Squires jogged onto the pitch, Berk ran with them, his face dripping with regurgitated potatoes.

"Lords and ladies, pages, squires and knights! Prithee let me bid you all the most hearty welcome to the first ever inter-school bladderball match!"

Lord de Beef's booming voice rang out over the crowd.

"Now may we all bellow a sporting Silveroaks welcome to our opponents – St Splendids School for the Financially Gifted!"

The St Splendids minstrels broke into an elaborate fanfare, which didn't quite drown out the cacophony of boos coming from the Silveroaks stalls.

Plucking something that may have been a piece of carrot from his eye, Berk watched the opposing team's portcullis rise. Then, through swirls of coloured smoke, the St Splendids team came striding out. Their red and gold armour sparkled. Then the captain stepped forwards.

"Which one of you is this 'Berserker' we keep hearing about?" he sneered.

Jax gave Berk a shove and the St Splendids captain looked disgusted.

"Is that a pea on your nose?"

14.

KICK OFF

"Prithee put your hands together and welcome our referee for today's match, Sir Donnick Remarque!" bellowed Lord de Beef.

Sir Donnick trotted onto the pitch. He carried his golden bugle in one hand, and the bladderball in the other. Then he blew a long blast on the bugle and tossed the bladderball into the air.

The big game had begun.

Berk squinted

into the sky and saw the bladderball hurtling towards him.

He held out his arms, and his world suddenly exploded into stars. A St Splendids player had made a lunging tackle, which knocked him flying.

Through the mud over his eyes, he saw a St Splendids girl launch the bladderball through a quintain.

PAAAARP! Went the trumpet.

"And what a splendiferous quintain hit from Elvira Golightly. That's 50 points for St Splendids!" boomed Lord de Beef. "Paggle caught a devastating tackle from

Brutus Spendthrift. I'll wager Brutus is relieved Berk hasn't got his catapult!"

There was a roar from the crowd, which became a chant: "Ber-serk-er, Ber-serk-er!"

Berk's head began to spin. He suddenly wished he was at home with Godwin and Warrick. They just liked him to be himself, not the Berserker. Berk realised how mean he had been to them.

"Yours Berk!"

The bladderball bounced off Berk's head. He caught it, then ran in the wrong direction. The next 20 minutes passed in a blur of mud, collisions and people angrily shouting his name.

When Sir Donnick blew the half-time bugle, Berk nearly wept with joy.

"That was some of the WORST bladderball playing I've ever seen!" Sir Kitt Trayning was trying to give everyone a half-time pep talk. But it was much more shouty than talky, and not really very peppy either.

"You lot couldn't even catch the plague! They're going to flatten us!"

"It's not over yet, Sir Kitt," said Jax. "We've still got the Paggle Pulcifier!"

Berk's face turned white and he reached for his helmet again.

Through the opening of the referee's tent, Warrick watched Sir Donnick Remarque practising his bugle poses in the mirror. Sir Donnick was too busy to notice Warrick slip inside and creep towards the bladderball.

Warrick dropped several black hairs onto the ball's surface:

**Wee-bag of warthog, good and fair,
Heed the owner of this hair.**

The bladderball began to twinkle with tiny silver stars.

15.

THE PHEASANTS TRIUMPH

Sir Donnick sounded a long blast on his bugle, and threw the bladderball in the air. The second half had begun. "You can do this," Jax hissed at Berk.

Berk watched the ball hurtle crazily upwards

before it came down
with a WHUMP – right
in his outstretched
arms. A St Splendids
sugger was pelting
towards him, and
in panic, Berk threw the
bladderball away and it hit
the sugger between his eyes.

The player tumbled
over and the bladderball
bounced back into
Berk's hands.

He lobbed it in the air and it flew into a quintain. "Ten points! That's more like it!" yelled Sir Kitt, and the crowd went ballistic.

Berk scored again a few minutes later – this time when he tripped over Gwen's ankle. Somehow he performed an impressive triple roll, released the bladderball in midair, and watched, astounded, as it hit a quintain.

As the quintain's sandbag swang around, it hit the St Splendids

captain, knocking him clean off his feet.
"Ber-ser-ker! Ber-ser-ker!" screamed
the crowd.

Berk stared at his hands. Something
weird was going on.

"Another 10 points for the Silveroaks
Squires! This is some truly magical
bladderball!" bellowed Lord de Beef.

The next 20 minutes were no different
and just as confusing. No matter how

badly Berk threw, the bladderball went exactly where he wanted.

He was relieved to hear Lord de Beef announce, "As we enter the last five minutes of the game, the score stands at 140, St Splendids and 90, the Silveroaks Squires."

For the final time, Sir Donnick launched the bladderball. The captain from St Splendids caught it and barked, "Did you really think you could beat us? You're nothing but peasants[20]."

"I ain't a pheasant." Big Wesley said, looking hurt.

Jax looked over at Sir Kitt, who nodded his head. It was time for the Paggle Pulcifier.

As the rest of the Silveroaks Squires got into formation, Berk gripped the bladderball and looked up. He could just make out his family high in the stalls, and he wondered where Godwin was.

"He should be here instead of me," thought Berk to himself. "I don't deserve this."

He looked at the bladderball and saw tiny stars twinkling around his hands.

What . . . ? Then he understood. Someone had enchanted it! He threw the ball away and watched as it flew straight for Sir Donnick Remarque, who dived face-first into the mud. The bladderball brushed the top of his head, taking his wig with it.

Then the bladderball, wearing the wig, hurtled straight for the prime quintain and struck it in the centre of the target.

For a moment the only sound was the rattle of the quintain spinning round on top of its pole. Then the crowd went completely bonkers.

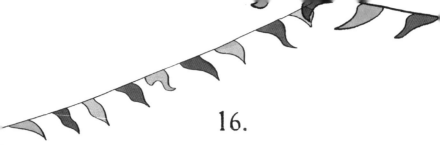

16.

TOADSTOOLS AND CROWNS

As Godwin hurried over the school drawbridge, he could hear the excited roar of the crowd. "I hope I'm not too late," he thought.

Everyone was standing around the winners' podium. The St Splendids team were clapping reluctantly and Lord de Beef was placing silver crowns on the winners' heads.

Godwin saw his Aunt Isobel, Uncle
Gregory and Patience at the front of the
stalls. They were wildly clapping. Near
them, Sir Donnick was suspiciously
examining the bladderball, while the
Silveroaks Squires
were red faced

with exhaustion and happiness.

But Berk didn't look happy.

He looked guilty. Was Warrick to blame for all of this?

Just as Lord de Beef placed the final crown on Berk, there was a loud screech;

CHEAT!

Sir Donnick was quivering with anger, his finger pointed at Berkley.

Lord de Beef looked furious. "Gadzooks, what fadoodle is this Sir Donnick? Prithee tell me thou hast proof?"

Sir Donnick strode forwards waving the bladderball in the air.

"This bladderball has been enchanted,

and I'll wager my bugle that it was Berkley Paggle!" With that, Sir Donnick began herding the Silveroak Squires down off the podium. "Come on you lot. You're all disqualified."

Jax and the rest of the team looked at Berk in disbelief. All Berk could do was raise his hands in a 'wasn't me' gesture.

Everyone really did think he was always responsible for this sort of thing.

"Come on Paggle!" snapped Sir Donnick. "Get off that podium!"

At that moment,

Warrick stepped out from behind the wooden fence where he had been hiding. At the same time, Godwin arrived breathlessly from around the corner. Warrick had taken a red toadstool from his robes and was crumbling it in his hands.

"Warrick, no!" yelled Godwin, but it was too late. As the toadstool spores rained onto the podium, there was a crackling fizz.

Then, with a loud WHOOOMPH, the podium disappeared along with Warrick, Godwin, Berk and the rest of the Silveroaks Squires. Sir Donnick was left spluttering in a cloud of purple smoke.

17.

KAPP ZLOCK

Berk wafted thick purple smoke away with his hand. As the air slowly cleared, he could see Godwin, Warrick and the Silveroaks Squires looking around in confusion.

They were in an underground cavern. Stalagmites protruded from the stone floor like dragon's teeth, and a thick layer of mist swirled around their feet. Godwin turned to Warrick.

"Warrick, what have you done?"

But before Warrick could explain, Gwen cried out.

"What is THAT?"

Everyone spun around. Looming out of the darkness was a huge, terrifying figure. Its face was hidden by a helmet with long antlers, and its fingers crackled with blue lightning.

"K-Kapp Zlock!" blurted Warrick.

The figure glided through the smoke.

"Warrick!" it boomed.

But Kapp Zlock was interrupted by a fierce cry from Godwin.

"Have at ye, white-liver!"

Godwin snapped off a nearby stalagmite and hurled it straight at the sorcerer.

At that moment, a small girl with bright red hair appeared.

"Noooooo!" she screamed. The stalagmite hit Kapp Zlock straight in the middle of his chest. He crumpled into a heap.

The girl stepped in front of Kapp Zlock. She raised her hands, which fizzed with blue light.

"Leave him alone!" she cried.

Warrick stepped forwards. "Willow?"

Just then, Kapp Zlock heaved himself upright. "I knew you'd find us, Warrick."

Warrick stared in astonishment. "D-Dad?"

Godwin gasped, and Berk peered out from behind a rock. "Will someone PLEASE tell me what is going on?"

Kapp Zlock pulled off the huge, antlered helmet. Underneath was the smiling face of Wenlock Pitchkettle.

"Dad! What the . . . ? How did . . . ? Zooks!" said Warrick.

"I should have told you, son," said Wenlock. "The Pitchkettle family has always had a very special duty. For thousands of years, one of us has taken the name of Kapp Zlock and defended the world from the horde."

"The horde?" spluttered Warrick.

"Yes, you know – assorted beings of great evil. Dragons, undead skeletons –

   that sort of thing.

"Up and down the land there are cracks in between our world and the horde's, which need to be maintained so that nothing gets out. Every now and then we have a little leak – remember that dragon last year?"

Everyone looked at Berk, who looked at his feet.

"Generally nothing goes wrong though. I wanted you and Willow to take over from me one day,

but your mum
thought it was too
dangerous. We were
always fighting about it.
In the end I promised her

I'd let Uncle Wylff take over.
We were going to open
up a little magic
shop instead.

"But when I came down here to make sure everything was ready for Wylff, Willow followed and accidentally shut the magic hatch behind her. We've been battling to keep the porthole shut ever since. I just hoped you'd find my book and work out what to do."

Willow beamed at her brother. "And you did! So where is all the stuff?"

Warrick slapped his forehead. "Oh THAT'S what that bit meant!"

Wenlock looked pained. "Do you mean you haven't brought the ingredients for the portal sealing spell?"

Suddenly there was a harsh rattling sound. Out of the darkness charged several skeletons waving rusty cutlasses and screeching, "AAAAARRRRRR!"

18.

THE PORTAL

"Pirate skeletons!" yelled Warrick and Willow's dad. "The horde is breaking through!" He struggled to get up, but immediately collapsed.

Godwin picked up both his stalagmites, and started whirling them round so fast they were blurs. He swung one into the nearest skeleton, which exploded in a shower of bones and rags. Jax, Big Wesley, Gwen and the La Forge twins did their best to hold off the others.

"We haven't got much time!" yelled Willow. "Follow me!"

She disappeared through an opening in the far side of the cavern. Godwin and Berk ran after her, followed by Warrick, who was helping his dad and the Silveroaks Squires, who had finished off the last pirate skeleton.

In the next chamber, everyone skidded to a halt. In front of them was a huge arch, filled with glowing light. Shrieks came from inside and bony arms reached out and grabbed at thin air. At the top was a small hole that spat blue lightning.

"We've got to do something!" yelled Willow, firing a blue ball of light at a goblin's head. "I can't believe you forgot the portal sealing ingredients, Warrick!"

Godwin started to bash at a leg bone, which was kicking wildly behind

the portal. "Warrick!" said Berk, "can you remember what the spell called for? Maybe we can find it all down here."

Warrick scrunched up his eyes. "Errrm, there was something about a ball of flesh I think . . . ?"

Everyone looked about wildly. There were plenty of bones on the floor, but there wasn't a scrap of flesh on any of them.

"Wait! What about this?" Jax held up the bladderball, which he had been holding ever since the match ended. "This is flesh isn't it?"

Warrick snapped his fingers.

"Of course! Wee-bag of warthog! That'll do!"

He recited the spell to himself under his breath. "Right, next we need a human tooth."

Gwendoline Trusskettle held up a tooth that she had found in a pile of bones. "Will this do?"

Warrick shook his head. "It might not be human!"

Big Wesley stepped forwards. "I'm a human ain't I?" He pulled up his top lip to reveal a gappy line of teeth.

Then he wriggled a loose tooth with his tongue. "I've got a wobbler. Might need a bit of help. Can you pull it out Jax?"

Jax looked up at his big friend uncertainly. "I might hurt you. What about you, Berserker?"

Berk hesitated.

Willow glanced
over impatiently. "Oh
for goodness'
sake," she said, and
then she shot an arc
of blue light from the
palm of her hand.
It exploded against Big
Wesley's tooth, which
neatly flew out and
landed in the dirt.

19.

THE UNSPOKEN TRUTH

"What's the last thing we need, Warrick?" asked Willow. The skull of what used to be a huge dog was trying to wrestle Godwin's stalagmite out of his hands. "Can you remember? Quickly!"

Warrick screwed up his eyes.

"AN UNSPOKEN TRUTH!
THAT'S THE LAST THING WE
NEED!"

Everyone looked around blankly. Willow
sent a bolt of lightening at a group of
green scorpions.

"Now's not the time to be shy!" She
yelled. "Someone must have a secret!"

Jax looked embarrassed, but held up
his hand. "Erm, I can't
get to sleep without my
Wommy."

"Wommy? Who's
she?" asked Berk.

"Wommy is a HE,"
snapped Jax. "And he's
a rabbit that my mum

knitted for me when I was little."

"Everyone know'sh about Wommy," lisped Big Wesley.

"Not good enough!" cried Warrick. "Anyone else?"

"I've got a crush on Big Wesley!" said Gwen.

"Eh?" said Big Wesley.

"I don't practise my lute every day!" interrupted Godwin. "AND I read Warrick's diary!"

"Oi!" said Warrick.

"It's no good – none of these are powerful enough!" yelled Willow. A huge, dark shape with large wings was becoming visible in the arch.

Berk looked at the portal, rigid with fear. Panicking, he suddenly blurted out:

I'M JEALOUS of GODWIN!

The portal seemed to judder, and the shrieks and cackles suddenly turned into moans.

"That's it!" shouted Warrick. "Keep going, Berk!"

Berk was now looking straight at Godwin. "I hated it when you arrived. You were so good at everything it made me look even more rubbish than usual. And then as soon as I got onto the bladderball team and was popular, you nearly completely ruined it with your stupid songs! I thought you couldn't bear me being good at something so you made up that stuff about Warrick!"

The moans behind the portal grew louder.

"It's working!" Wenlock shouted. "More!"

Godwin looked at his cousin. "Well, I'm jealous of you too! I miss my mum and dad so much, but you get to see yours all the time! Plus I haven't got any brothers or sisters but YOU have! Patience is great but you're just mean to her all the time! AND you're amazing at building things – I've no idea how you made that catapult, let alone defeated a dragon with it. I'd love to be able to do something like that!"

Berk looked flabbergasted. "Really?" .

Just then, there was a deep groaning sound from the portal.

"They're weakening! Throw in the tooth!" cried Wenlock.

Big Wesley flung the tooth into the pulsating light of the arch. There was a huge inward rush of air, and loose bones were sucked towards the portal.

The massive shape behind the vortex thrashed wildly. Willow looked at the hole above the arch. It was spewing out lightning.

"That's the lock!" she cried. "You need to plug it with the ball of flesh!"

Berk peered above him. "How are we going to get the bladderball up there?

"This is a job for the Berserker," said Jax. "Just imagine it's a quintain."

"But that's twice as high!" spluttered Berk. "Besides, Warrick had enchanted the ball."

Warrick looked at his father. "Can I enchant it again?"

Wenlock shook his head.

"The magic from the portal would overpower the spell."

Berk looked up at the hole and thought hard. "We could try the Paggle Pulcifier?"

"The what?" asked Willow.

Wesley and Jax were already getting into position. Jax yelled over to the others, "Gwen! You and the twins need to make sure nothing gets through the portal!"

Jax looked at Berk.

"You ready Berserker?" he said.

Berk gulped.

The shape behind the vortex thrashed its huge tail.

"OK, do it!" screamed Willow.

Taking a deep breath, Berk sped towards Jax and Big Wesley. As he ran up their backs, Gwen threw him the bladderball, which he caught. As Jax and Wesley threw him in the air, Warrick and Willow shot out blue beams of light, which gave him a little more height. Just before he began to fall, Berk threw the bladderball with all his might. Everyone held their breath as the ball disappeared into the smoke and lightning, and then with a sudden POP it plugged the hole. As Berk crashed to the floor, a silence fell over the cavern, and the light in the arch disappeared in wisps of smoke.

20.

BACK TO NORMAL

A huge green dragon made from jelly quivered gently at the centre of the table. Gregory and Isobel had laid on a great feast at their castle to celebrate Willow and Wenlock's safe return. Everyone helped themselves to large bowls of fermenty[21], while plates piled high with spiced meats and vegetables billowed clouds of steam into the rafters of the great hall.

Despite the pain in his leg, which was encased in a hardened mixture of flour and egg whites, Berk grinned.

"That was pretty impressive throw with the stalagmite, Godwin!" said Wenlock, who was sitting on the dais next to Berk, his chest wrapped in bandages. "Are you sure you don't want to defend the world from the evil horde when you're a knight?"

"No thanks Mr Pitchkettle," said Godwin. "I'll need to get home and help my parents."

"I've got so many great ideas for our magic shop, Dad!" Said Warrick. "I've made some unbreakable enchanted glasses! I can't see a thing through them yet, but they're strong as an oxen!"

"Plenty of time for that later son," said Wenlock, winking at Hildred.

Hildred smiled at her husband and

squeezed Willow's shoulder.

"I'm just looking forward to going back to school!" interrupted Willow. "It was pretty boring being stuck in that cavern fighting evil creatures all day. I'm going to be top of the class in everything!"

Godwin looked at Willow with panic in his eyes. "But I'M top of the—"

Isobel interrupted Godwin quickly. "Well I for one think you all need a quiet term. Your knight training has suffered terribly, and I can't remember the last time either of you helped me muck out the stables."

"You're right Aunt Isobel," agreed Godwin. "We'll have a quiet term, and really knuckle down with our studies." He cast a defiant glance at Willow.

Berk nodded in agreement. "Yep – a nice quiet term. No more dragons, no more bladderball, no more magic and definitely no more stupid jealous rivalries."

"No more bladderball?" exclaimed Jax, through a mouthful of cabbage. "Well there'll be a space for Godwin and Warrick on the team then. You two were proper killbucks down there!"

"Yeah – amathing knight thkillth," nodded Big Wesley.

"I think this calls for a ballad," said Godwin, producing his lute.

"We're joining in!" said Jax.

Coz this is the story of
Berk the Berserker,
who blocked up a portal,
so the baddies couldn't hurt ya.
With big G for the win
and Warrick the little wizard,
and Willow with her magic boltz,
she was firing up a blizzard.
※
Those skeletons and evil beasts
were no match for these heroes.
Big Wesley lost a favourite tooth.
We aint no loser zeroes!

The squires are the toughest team,
we'll leave you in a puddle.
We'll save you when it all goes wrong,
and the world gets in a muddle.

So whenever you've got scorpions
or dragons to be pounded . . .

. . . then go and bother someone else.
These heroes are all grounded.

The
End

GLOSSARY

Some words from the medieval times are different from words today and no one uses them now . . . maybe they should?

1. Hose — MEDIEVAL UNDERWEAR OR TROUSERS

2. Bubonic — BUBONIC PLAGUE WAS A NASTY DISEASE

3. Mummers — TRAVELLING ACTORS

4. Chivalry — MEDIEVAL CODE OF HONOUR AND VIRTUE

5. Fauntkins — CHILDREN

6. Squiddle — WASTE TIME

7. Privy — TOILET

8. Frushed — TO CRUSH OR BREAK

9. Killbuck — FIERCE PERSON

10. Huddermudder — SECRET

11. Trencher — MEDIEVAL PLATE, USUALLY MADE FROM A DISC OF STALE BREAD.

12. Fadoodle — NONSENSE

13. Fopdoodle — INSIGNIFICANT PERSON

14. Scroggling — LAST APPLE ON THE TREE

15. Braggart — BOASTFUL PERSON

16. Bellytimber — FOOD

17. Swerk — BECOME TROUBLED

18. Carked — WORRIED

19. Pottage — MEDIEVAL SOUP, USUALLY MADE FROM VEGETABLES.

20. Peasants — POOR MEDIEVAL FARM LABOURERS

21. Fermenty — A KIND OF PORRIDGE MADE FROM WHEAT

COMING SOON!

GOOD KNIGHT, BAD KNIGHT AND THE FLYING MACHINE

This term, Berk (Bad Knight), Godwin (Good Knight) and Warrick are working on a flying machine.

Their test flights always seem to end in disaster though, so the boys try to enlist the help of Warrick's supremely talented sister, Willow. But Willow is more interested in taming an irate, stinky dragon with a dangerous grudge . . .

Hold onto your helmets for a new armour rattling adventure from Tom Knight!